Phonics Friends

Amy's Big Race
The Sound of Long **A**

The
**Child's
World**

By Cecilia Minden and Joanne Meier

The Child's World

Published in the United States of America
by The Child's World®
PO Box 326
Chanhassen, MN 55317-0326
800-599-READ
www.childsworld.com

A special thank you to Gabriel Onyema and the girls
who ran with her in the "big race!" And to Mrs. Bedar
and Mrs. Robinson for allowing us to photograph at
Shoesmith Elementary School.

The Child's World®: Mary Berendes, Publishing Director

Editorial Directions, Inc.: E. Russell Primm, Editorial
Director and Project Editor; Katie Marsico, Associate
Editor; Judith Shiffer, Associate Editor and School Media
Specialist; Linda S. Koutris, Photo Researcher and
Selector

The Design Lab: Kathleen Petelinsek, Design and Page
Production

Photographs ©: Photo setting and photography by Romie
and Alice Flanagan/Flanagan Publishing Services.

Library of Congress Cataloging-in-Publication Data
Minden, Cecilia.
  Amy's big race : the sound of long A / by Cecilia
Minden and Joanne Meier.
    p. cm. — (Phonics friends)
  Summary: Simple text featuring the long "a" sound
describes how Amy and other girls run a race around
the lake.
  ISBN 1-59296-317-X (library bound : alk. paper)
[1. English language—Phonetics. 2. Reading.] I. Meier,
Joanne D. II. Title. III. Series.
  PZ7.M6539Am 2004
  [E]—dc22   2004002231

Note to parents and educators:
The Child's World® has created Phonics Friends with the goal of exposing children to engaging stories and pictures that assist in phonics development. The books in the series will help children learn the relationships between the letters of written language and the individual sounds of spoken language. This contact helps children learn to use these relationships to read and write words.

The books in this series follow a similar format. An introductory page, to be read by an adult, introduces the child to the phonics feature, or sound, that will be highlighted in the book. Read this page to the child, stressing the phonic feature. Help the student learn how to form the sound with her mouth. The Phonics Friends story and engaging photographs follow the introduction. At the end of the story, word lists categorize the feature words into their phonic element. Additional information on using these lists is on The Child's World® Web site listed at the top of this page.

Each book in this series has been carefully written to meet specific readability requirements. Close attention has been paid to elements such as word count, sentence length, and vocabulary. Readability formulas measure the ease with which the text can be read and understood. Each Phonics Friends book has been analyzed using the Spache readability formula. For more information on this formula, as well as the levels for each of the books in this series please visit The Child's World® Web site.

Reading research suggests that systematic phonics instruction can greatly improve students' word recognition, spelling, and comprehension skills. The Phonics Friends series assists in the teaching of phonics by providing students with important opportunities to apply their knowledge of phonics as they read words, sentences, and text.

The letter a makes two sounds.

The short sound of *a* sounds like *a* as in:

 cat and *add*.

The long sound of *a* sounds like *a* as in:

 cake and *date*.

In this book, you will read words that have the long *a* sound as in:

 race, lake, waves, and *place.*

Today is the big race.

Amy is in the race.

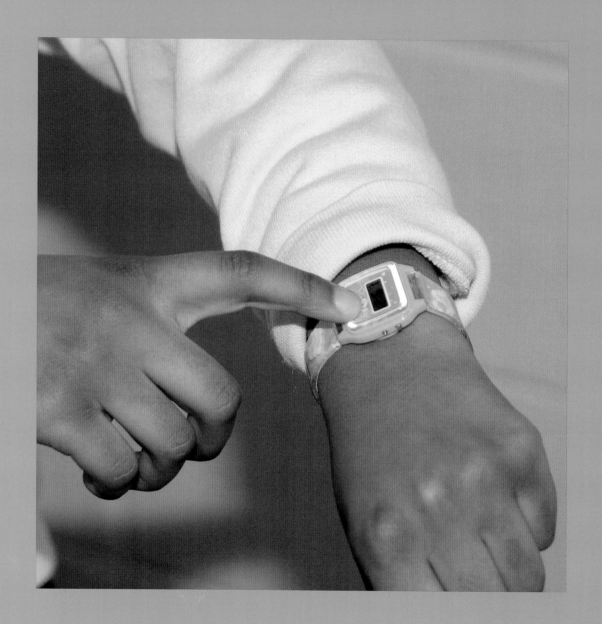

She wakes up early.

She can't be late!

The race is around the lake.

Amy hopes she wins the race!

Akisha Wilson
Amy Tate
Bedara P...
Betsy Tyler
Carlotta Diaz
Donata Hyranski
Eva Goldman
Isabel Perez
Monique Parker
Noriko Fujimora
Rose WhiteFeather
Tanisha Johnson
Wan Lee

Race :

Monday

Amy goes to the gate.

Her name is on the list.

Amy waves to her friends.

They came to watch.

Amy takes her place in line.

They all begin to race.

The girls run fast around the lake. Amy takes the lead. She runs very fast.

Will she win?

Will she take first place?

Amy wins the race!

She has a big smile

on her face!

Fun Facts

Did you know that Lake Baikal is the deepest lake in the world and is located in Russia? Lake Superior is the largest freshwater lake in the world and touches the states of Michigan, Wisconsin, Minnesota, and part of Canada. The Dead Sea in Israel is called a sea but is actually a lake. It is the lowest lake in the world. It is also the saltiest—hardly any plants or animals are able to live in it!

You have to be a great runner to compete in some races! Long-distance races are called marathons. They date back to the Olympic Games held in Athens, Greece, in the late 1800s. The oldest and most famous marathon is the Boston Marathon. It is run in Boston, Massachusetts. Runners travel more than 26 miles (42 kilometers) in this race.

Activity

A Picnic by the Lake

If the weather is warm and sunny, pack a picnic basket with your family and head toward the shore of a nearby lake. Don't forget to bring a blanket, sunscreen lotion, and your favorite foods. Some activities you could try include swimming, fishing, or going for a boat ride.

To Learn More

Books
About the Sound of Long A
Flanagan, Alice K. *Play Day: The Sound of Long A*. Chanhassen, Minn.: The Child's World, 2000.

About Lakes
Fowler, Allan. *It Could Still Be a Lake*. Danbury, Conn.: Children's Press, 1996.
McCully, Emily Arnold. *Grandmas at the Lake: Stories and Pictures*. New York: Harper & Row, 1990.
Say, Allen. *The Lost Lake*. Boston: Houghton Mifflin, 1989.

About Races
Augarde, Steve. *Vroom! Vroom!: A Pop-Up Race to the Finish*. Boston: Little, Brown, 2001.
Brown, Marc Tolon. *Arthur's Reading Race*. New York: Random House, 1995.
Pruett, Judy, Scott Pruett, and Mike Dietz (illustrator). *Twelve Little Race Cars*. Granite Bay, Calif.: Word Weaver Books, 1998.

Web Sites
Visit our home page for lots of links about the Sound of Long A:

http://www.childsworld.com/links.html

Note to Parents, Teachers, and Librarians: We routinely check our Web links to make sure they're safe, active sites—so encourage your readers to check them out!

Long A
Feature Words

Proper Names

Amy

**Feature Words with the
Consonant-Vowel-Silent E
Pattern**

came
face
gate
lake
late
race
take
wake
wave

**Feature Words with Other
Long Vowel Pattern**

today

About the Authors

*Cecilia Minden, PhD,
directs the Language and
Literacy Program at the
Harvard Graduate School
of Education. She is a
reading specialist with
classroom and administrative experience in
grades K–12. She earned her PhD in reading
education from the University of Virginia.
Cecilia and her husband Dave Cupp enjoy
sharing their love of reading with their
granddaughter Chelsea.*

*Joanne Meier, PhD, has
worked as an elementary
school teacher and
university professor. She
earned her BA in early
childhood education from
the University of South Carolina, and her MEd
and PhD in education from the University
of Virginia. She currently works as a literacy
consultant for schools and private organizations.
Joanne Meier lives with her husband Eric,
and spends most of her time chasing her two
daughters, Kella and Erin, and her two cats,
Sam and Gilly, in Charlottesville, Virginia.*